KU-305-641

CONTENTS

NEW DAWN PRESS

So much to
READ

Delightful Stories

The Ugly Duckling

In the middle of a forest there was a large lake. Many birds lived near this lake. In the hot afternoon, the animals came to drink water from it.

Mamma Duck also lived near the lake. One day, she flapped her wings and came rushing to the other birds.

"I've just laid seven eggs," she said. "Oh, I'm so excited! Soon they will hatch, and I'll have seven little ducklings."

"That's wonderful," said the other birds.

Mamma Duck sat on the eggs every day and waited for them to hatch.

A few weeks later, the eggs began to hatch. Mamma Duck watched lovingly as each shell cracked and a tiny little duckling poked its way out of the shell.

At first, each duckling tapped at the shell with its bill and cracked it. Then it poked its bill out of the shell and soon the rest of the body wiggled out too.

One by one, all the little ducklings crawled out and began quacking. They had soft white feathers and bright eyes. Only one little duckling looked different from the rest.

Soon the forest was filled with the quack quack of the seven hungry ducklings.

Mamma Duck looked at her little brood proudly. How lovely they were!

"Yes, my dears, I know you're hungry," she said. "You shall have seeds and insects to eat. And when you're a little older, I'll teach you how to find your own food. But first, let me clean you up a bit. You are all wet and sticky."

She made all the ducklings stand in line. One by one, she went to each duckling and gently wiped its feathers. The ducklings quacked softly and cuddled up to her soft body as she wiped them clean.

When Mamma Duck came to the last little duckling, she quacked in surprise.

"What an ugly little thing you are!" said Mamma Duck. "You don't even look like the others. How did you come here?"

The poor little duckling was hurt and sad. Why did his mother say he was ugly?

"I'm your baby, Mother," he said, trying to cuddle up to her.

"Go away!" quacked Mamma Duck. "You can't be my baby. The egg you came from must have rolled into my nest by mistake. My ducklings are so pretty. Just look at you!"

"Go away! Go away!" quacked the other ducklings. "You are not one of us."

Mamma Duck gathered up her little brood and waddled away. The poor little duckling stood there sadly.

"Nobody loves me," he sighed. "I wonder whose baby I am. Where is my mother?"

He walked through the forest, looking for his mother. He walked and he walked on his tiny feet till he had left the forest far behind.

There was a road that led out of the forest. The duckling walked along that road, looking around him. Soon he came to a large farm. There were goats grazing on the green grass. He decided to look for his mother on the farm.

The poor little duckling walked around the farm till he met a turkey. She had bright, colourful feathers and was eating some berries.

"Are you my mother?" asked the duckling, looking up at the turkey.

"No, I'm not your mother," said the turkey. "Just look at your feathers — they're so plain and ugly. How can you be my baby?"

"I can't find my mother," said the poor little duckling. "Maybe she is on this farm. Will you help me look for her?"

"No, I won't," said the turkey rudely. "Now go away. You are so ugly."

The poor duckling turned away sadly.

He walked along till he saw a hen with her brood of little chicks.

"Cluck! Cluck!" said the hen. "Come along, let me teach you how to dig for worms."

She pecked at the mud with her beak. Soon she had caught a wiggling worm. She fed it to one of the chicks. Just then the little duckling came up to them.

"Have you lost a baby?" he asked the hen.

"No, my babies are all here," the hen answered.

"I can't find my mother," said the duckling.

"I'm sorry about that," clucked the hen.

The poor little duckling sighed and walked ahead. Soon his little feet began to ache.

"I'll just rest for a while below this tree," he said. "Then I'll go looking for my mother again."

He shut his eyes and soon fell asleep.

"Cock a doodle doo!" crowed a cock sitting on the tree.

The little duckling woke up with a start. He looked up and saw the cock crowing loudly.

"Cock a doodle doo! Tell me, who are you?"

"I'm a poor little duckling. I have lost my mother. Have you seen her anywhere?" asked the duckling.

"No, I have not," answered the cock.

The duckling walked on till he came to the edge of the farm. He saw a peacock dancing about with his beautiful feathers spread out.

The duckling walked up to the peacock and said, "Am I your baby?"

The peacock tossed his head proudly and said, "How can you be my baby? Just look at yourself. You are so plain and ugly. You do not have beautiful feathers like mine."

And the peacock turned this way and that, showing off his colourful feathers. Then he took pity on the duckling and said, "Don't worry. I'm sure you'll find out whose baby you are."

The duckling put his head down and walked back along the path he had come.

"It's no use," he sobbed. "I'll never find my mother. I'll have to grow up all by myself. Nobody wants me, because I'm plain and ugly."

A macaw was perched on a tree nearby. She heard the little duckling sobbing.

"What's the matter? Why are you crying?" she asked.

"I've lost my mother," said the duckling. "I don't know who she is. Are you my mother?"

"Don't be silly!" said the macaw. "Just look at my colourful feathers. How can I be your mother? Run along now."

The poor little duckling walked on.

'I'd better go back to the forest,' he said to himself.

Just then he heard a tinkling sound and looked around. He saw a cow grazing quietly in the field. As she turned her head from side to side to shoo away the flies, the bell around her neck tinkled softly.

The duckling walked up to her and said, "I'm looking for my mother. Are you my mother?"

The cow laughed and said, "Do you see my big horns and my long tail? How can I be your mother? You don't look like me."

The duckling walked on till he reached the edge of the forest. It was cool and shady here, and the birds cheeped as they flew about.

As the duckling walked along, he saw a monkey swinging from branch to branch.

"Where are you off to, little one?" asked the monkey.

"I'm looking for my mother," said the duckling. "I can't find her anywhere. Are you my mother?"

The monkey laughed loudly.

"What a foolish little duckling you are! Don't you know I am a monkey? How can I be your mother? Go away."

The duckling shook his head sadly and went on his way. He walked slowly along a path that went through the forest. It was a hot day, and he was tired and thirsty. Suddenly he saw a pool of water shining in the sun. He quickly walked up to it to drink some water.

As he bent his head to drink, he saw his reflection in the water.

"Just look at me! How ugly I am!" he said. "No wonder no one wants to be my mother. Maybe that's why my mother left me and went away. She thought I was too ugly."

A swan was standing nearby. She heard the duckling's words and turned around.

As soon as she saw the duckling, she rushed to him and hugged him.

"There you are, my poor lost baby!" she said. "I've been looking for you everywhere."

The duckling looked at the swan in wonder.

"Am I ... am I really your baby?" he asked.

"Yes, you are, my dear," said the swan.

"But I'm so ugly and you are so beautiful," said the duckling.

The swan laughed and kissed her baby tenderly.

"Who says you are ugly? You are the most beautiful baby in the whole world. And when you grow up, you shall be a beautiful swan."

LEARN TO SAY THESE WORDS

flapped	mistake
excited	sighed
hatch	grazing
cracked	brood
wiggled	pecked
feathers	colourful
different	perched
cuddled	swinging
lovingly	foolish
surprise	tenderly

CAN YOU NAME THESE PICTURES?

Snow White

In a kingdom far away, there lived a king and queen who were wise and kind. All the people in the kingdom loved them.

Only one thing made the king and queen unhappy. They had no children.

One day, as the queen sat sewing, she pricked her finger on the needle. A drop of red blood fell on the white cloth she was sewing.

"I wish I had a baby girl with skin as white as snow and lips as red as blood!" she sighed.

A few months later, a lovely baby girl was born to her, with skin as white as snow.

The king and queen were delighted. They named the baby Snow White.

When Snow White was still a little girl, her mother died. The king married again, so that Snow White would have a mother to love her.

But the new queen cared only for herself, and wanted to be the most beautiful lady in the kingdom. She had a magic mirror. Every day, she would stand before it and ask,

"Mirror, mirror on the wall,

Who is the fairest of us all?"

And the mirror would reply,

"You, my queen, are the fairest of all."

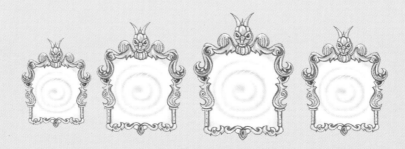

As the years went by, little Snow White grew up into a beautiful young girl. She was helpful and kind and all the people in the kingdom loved her.

A few years later, the king died, and Snow White was left all alone. Her new mother did not love her and was jealous of her beauty.

One day, the new queen stood before her magic mirror and asked,

"Mirror, mirror on the wall,

Who is the fairest of us all?"

But this time, the mirror replied,

"Snow White is the fairest of all."

This made the queen very angry. She had watched Snow White grow from a pretty little child into a lovely young girl. And now the mirror said she was the fairest in the kingdom!

"I must get rid of her," she said.

She called for her chief huntsman and said to him, "Take Snow White deep into the forest and kill her."

The huntsman was amazed.

"But . . . but . . . she is only a young girl! What has she done, my queen?" he asked.

"That is not for you to know. Just do as I tell you," replied the queen sternly.

The next morning, the huntsman took Snow White into the forest with a heavy heart.

"Where are we going?" asked Snow White.

"Wait and see, dear," said the huntsman, wondering how he was going to kill this lovely young girl.

They went deeper and deeper into the forest. Then the huntsman stopped and turned to Snow White.

"I want to tell you something," he said gently. "The queen does not like you. She has ordered me to bring you here and kill you. But I cannot kill you, so please run away and do not come back to the kingdom ever again."

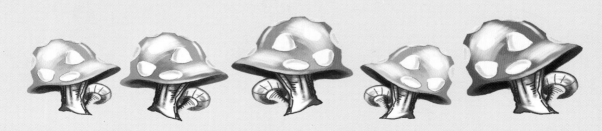

"But what have I done?" asked Snow White. "Why doesn't the queen like me?"

"I don't know," replied the huntsman. "But please go away and never come back again."

"Thank you for sparing my life," said Snow White. She kissed the huntsman and then walked deeper into the forest.

The huntsman told the queen that he had carried out her orders.

Meanwhile, Snow White walked and walked till she came to a tiny cottage.

'I wonder who lives here?' she said to herself. 'Maybe I can rest here for a while.'

Snow White knocked on the cottage door, but there was no reply. She saw that the door was not locked, so she opened it and went in.

She found some candles near the door and lit them. In the candlelight, she saw a small table with seven tiny chairs placed around it. There were seven small plates and a bowl of fruit on the table.

She went upstairs and found seven small beds placed in a row.

"Oh, I'm so tired. I think I will sleep here for a while," she said.

Then she lay down across the beds and was soon fast asleep.

The little cottage belonged to seven dwarfs. They worked in a gold mine at the edge of the forest.

That evening, when they returned home, they saw lights shining in the windows.

"Someone is in our house," said Grumpy. "How did they get in?"

"Sleepy must have forgotten to lock the door again," said Doc.

"But it was Dopey's turn to lock the door," said Sleepy.

"Atishoo!" said Sneezy. "I'm catching a cold out here while all of you are fighting."

The dwarfs went in and looked around. When they went upstairs, they were surprised to find a beautiful young girl fast asleep on their beds.

"Who is this?" asked Bashful.

"How did she get here?" Happy asked.

"Let's wake her up, and then we'll know," said Grumpy.

"No, no, let her sleep," said Sleepy.

But Snow White woke up when she heard the dwarfs talking among themselves.

"Who are you?" asked Dopey.

"My name is Snow White," she said.

"Have you lost your way?" asked Happy.

Then Snow White told the dwarfs her sad story. They were very angry when they heard that the wicked queen had tried to kill the lovely young girl.

"Now I have no home," said Snow White.

"Don't worry," said Dopey. "You can stay with us. You will be safe here."

So Snow White began to live in the cottage. Every morning, after the dwarfs left for work, she cleaned the house and cooked the meals. They told her not to open the door to anyone else.

Back in the castle, the wicked queen was happy that she was once more the most beautiful lady in the land.

One day, as she was passing the magic mirror, she asked,

"Mirror, mirror on the wall,

Who is the fairest of us all?"

To her amazement, the mirror replied,

"Snow White is still the fairest in the land, my queen. She lives in a cottage deep in the forest."

In the mirror, the queen saw Snow White singing happily as she cleaned the cottage.

The queen was very angry.

"So the huntsman lied to me!" she said. "Snow White is not dead. Never mind. This time I shall kill her myself."

The queen dressed up as an old woman and put some poisoned apples in a basket. Then she set off for the cottage in the forest.

When she knocked on the door, Snow White asked, "Who is it?"

"Just an old fruit seller," said the queen.

"I don't need any fruit," said Snow White. "Besides, I cannot open the door to anybody."

The queen went round to the window and showed a juicy red apple to Snow White.

"I am sure you will love this apple," she said. "Why don't you just take a bite and see?"

As soon as Snow White bit into the apple, she fell down dead. The queen cackled wickedly and went away.

When the dwarfs returned, they were surprised that Snow White did not open the door.

They climbed in through the window and found her lying dead on the floor.

"I knew we shouldn't have left her alone in the house," sobbed Sleepy.

"It must have been the wicked queen," growled Grumpy. "I wish I could kill her."

The dwarfs placed Snow White in a glass coffin and kept it in the garden.

One day, a prince passing by, saw the lovely girl in the coffin and fell in love with her.

"Who is she?" he asked the dwarfs.

They told him Snow White's sad story.

"May I kiss her?" asked the prince.

"Yes, you may," the dwarfs said.

Just as the prince lifted Snow White from the coffin, a piece of the apple fell out of her mouth. Snow White came to life again. She saw the prince and fell in love with him. Soon they were married and lived happily ever after.

LEARN TO SAY THESE WORDS

unhappy

knocked

sewing

castle

pricked

delighted

mirror

magic

fairest

jealous

amazed

sternly

angry

beautiful

wondering

ordered

forgotten

belonged

poisoned

climbed

CAN YOU NAME THESE PICTURES?

Hansel and Gretel

Once upon a time, a poor woodcutter lived at the edge of a forest with his wife and two children. Though they were poor, they were very happy together. Every morning, the woodcutter went into the forest to cut wood. Sometimes, his children Hansel and Gretel went with him. They helped him tie the logs of wood into bundles to sell at the market.

When Hansel and Gretel were still young, their mother died. They were very sad and missed her a lot. Their father decided to marry again, so that Hansel and Gretel would have a mother to love them and care for them.

But their new mother did not care for them at all. She did not like being poor.

"We never have enough to eat," she said to the woodcutter one night.

"What can I do?" sighed the woodcutter. "It is so hard to earn enough money to feed my family."

"I have an idea," said his wife. "Let us take the children into the forest tomorrow and leave them there."

"How can I do that?" said the woodcutter.

"You must," said his wife.

Hansel was standing near the door. He heard his stepmother's cruel words.

Hansel crept out of the house and picked up some pebbles. He hid them in his pocket.

The next morning, their father and stepmother took them into the forest. Hansel walked slowly behind the others and dropped the pebbles, one by one, along the path.

Gretel turned around and asked, "What are you doing, Hansel?"

"Shh!" whispered Hansel. "I'm dropping pebbles so that we can find our way home."

"But why do we need to find the way back home?" asked Gretel.

"I'll tell you later," said Hansel. "Now keep on walking."

When they came to the middle of the forest, their stepmother stopped and said, "Children, you must wait here. Your father and I have to go deeper into the forest to gather wood. We will come back later and take you home with us. Here is some bread for you to eat."

Hansel turned to his father. But his father could not bear to look at him. He placed his hand on Gretel's head for a moment and then began walking quickly into the forest.

Gretel sat down to wait under a tree. Hansel watched as their father and stepmother went deeper into the forest.

The children waited all day long. When they began to feel hungry, they ate the slice of dry bread that their stepmother had given them.

Soon it began to get dark.

"Hansel, why hasn't Father come to take us home?" asked Gretel.

"He will, Gretel, don't worry," said Hansel. But he knew their parents would not come.

After a while, Gretel began to cry.

"Don't cry, Gretel," said Hansel. "Look, here are the pebbles I dropped along the path this morning. Now we can find our way home with the help of the pebbles."

When Hansel and Gretel reached home, their father was very happy to see them.

Their stepmother was very angry, but she did not want to show it.

"Where were you, children?" she asked. "How did you find your way home?"

"We waited for you till it began to get dark," said Gretel. "Then we came home on our own."

"I had dropped some pebbles along the path we took in the morning," said Hansel. "We found our way back home with their help."

That night, their stepmother told their father, "We must take them deeper into the woods tomorrow."

Once again, Hansel heard these words. He decided to go out and gather pebbles.

But when he tried to open the door, he found it was locked! Hansel sat on his bed and thought hard till he had an idea.

The next morning, their stepmother woke them up and gave each of them a slice of bread for breakfast. Hansel hid his slice in his pocket.

"We have to go to the forest again, children," said their stepmother. "This time, please stay where I leave you. Don't try to come home on your own. Wait for us. We will bring you back."

They walked along the path that led through the forest. It was a fine day. The birds sang in the trees and colourful butterflies flitted here and there. It was cool and shady in the forest.

Gretel skipped along happily, chattering with her father. Hansel walked behind the others. His stepmother looked back from time to time and said, "Hurry up, Hansel. Why are you walking so slowly?"

Hansel began walking faster. As he walked, he dropped crumbs of bread behind him to mark the way home.

Their father and stepmother led them deeper into the forest. They stopped at an open place with trees on all sides.

"You must wait here till we return," said their stepmother.

Their father hugged both of them and walked away quickly. Once more, the children waited while their parents gathered wood. Once more, their parents did not return.

Hansel began looking for the crumbs of bread to help them find their way home. But he could not see any. The birds had eaten up all the crumbs! Gretel began to cry.

"How will we find our way home now, Hansel?" she asked.

"Don't cry, Gretel," said Hansel. "I'm sure we'll find someone to take us home."

The children walked on and on till they came to a strange house. It was made of bread and cake. The door and roof were made of chocolate and the walls were made of pink icing.

Hansel broke off a piece of the wall and ate it. Gretel ate a piece of the window. Soon they were merrily eating up bits of the house.

"Mmm, this tastes wonderful," said Hansel. "I wonder whose house this is."

The house belonged to a wicked witch who ate little children. She had made the house with bread and cake so that children would come to eat it. Then she would catch them and eat them up.

When the witch heard the children talking, she came out and said in a sweet voice, "Come in, my dear little children. You look tired and hungry."

As soon as the children went into the house, the witch pounced on Hansel and locked him up in a cage. Then she made Gretel cook the food and do all the work in the house.

The witch wanted to make Hansel fat before eating him. So she gave him plenty of food to eat. Poor Gretel got very little food. Hansel saved up his food to share with her.

Every day, the witch would tell Hansel, "Show me your finger. Are you fat enough for me to eat now?"

Hansel would show the witch a small bone. The witch could not see very well. She would feel the bone with her fingers and say, "No, you are not fat enough yet."

Every day, the witch came to see if Hansel was fat enough. When she felt the bone, she would go away.

Then one day, the witch said, "I cannot wait any longer. I shall eat the boy today."

Hansel and Gretel trembled in fear. The witch told Gretel to light the fire to heat the oven. Gretel wondered what she could do to save her brother.

Suddenly she had an idea. She turned to the witch and said, "Will you please see if the oven is hot enough?"

The witch opened the oven door and leaned in to see if it was hot enough.

In a flash, Gretel pushed her into the oven. The wicked witch was burnt to death.

Then Gretel let Hansel out of the cage.

"What a brave and clever girl you are!" said Hansel, hugging his sister.

They found a box full of gold coins hidden under the witch's bed. They took it with them and went out into the forest once more. A little bird flew up to them and showed them the way out of the forest. When they reached home, their father rushed out to meet them.

"Oh, I'm so glad you're safe!" he said. "Your stepmother is dead. Now we can all live together happily."

The children gave their father the box of gold and they lived happily ever after.

LEARN TO SAY THESE WORDS

together	gathered
idea	strange
cruel	merrily
pebbles	wicked
whispered	pounced
wondered	belonged
slice	trembled
colourful	leaned
flitted	flash
deeper	burnt

CAN YOU NAME THESE PICTURES?

Chicken Licken

In a forest far away lived a foolish little chick called Chicken Licken. He was afraid of everything. If he heard the sound of thunder, he would rush to hide below a bush. If the crows cawed loudly, he would jump up in fear. When the wind blew through the trees with a rushing sound, he trembled and ran about, looking for a place to hide.

But more than anything else, there was one thing that always worried Chicken Licken. He was afraid that, one day, the sky would fall on his head.

One bright sunny morning, Chicken Licken wandered through the forest looking for food. He poked about in the mud here and there, and ate the juicy worms and seeds that he found.

"Mmm ... that was quite a nice meal," said Chicken Licken after a while. "Now I shall have a nap under this shady oak tree."

He sat down below the tree and went to sleep. After a while, an acorn fell from the tree and landed on his head.

Chicken Licken woke up with a start.

"Ouch! What was that?" he wondered. He looked up and cried out, "The sky is falling down. I knew it! I must go and tell the king."

Chicken Licken rushed off to find the king. He did not know where the king lived.

"I'm sure he lives in the middle of the forest," he said, as he ran along.

Soon he met Henny Penny, who was clucking away as she looked for seeds.

"Where are you going in such a hurry?" asked Henny Penny.

"The sky is falling down," gasped Chicken Licken. "I'm rushing off to find the king so that I can tell him."

"Is that so? Then I'll come with you," said Henny Penny.

As they hurried along, they came across Cocky Locky.

"Cock-a-doodle-doo! Where are you off to?" he asked in surprise.

"Don't you know? The sky is falling down!" said Henny Penny.

"How can that be?" asked Cocky Locky.

"It's true. A piece of it fell on my head when I was sleeping," said Chicken Licken.

"Dear me! What shall we do now?" asked Cocky Locky.

"We're off to tell the king. Why don't you come with us?" said Chicken Licken.

So Chicken Licken, Henny Penny and Cocky Locky rushed off to find the king.

On the way, they met Ducky Lucky, who was standing near a pond.

"What's happening? Why are all of you rushing like this?" he asked.

"We're going to find the king," said Cocky Locky.

"The sky is falling down," gasped Henny Penny. "Chicken Licken saw it."

"Oh my goodness!" said Ducky Lucky. "I'll go along with you."

He waddled along with them.

As they ran along, they saw Drakey Lakey swimming in the pond.

"Quack! Quack! What's the matter? Is the forest on fire?" he asked.

"No, it's much worse than that," gasped Ducky Lucky. "The sky is falling down."

"So we're going to tell the king," said Henny Penny.

"Do you know where he lives?" asked Drakey Lakey, as he waddled up to them.

"No, but I think he lives in the middle of the forest," said Chicken Licken.

"I'll go with you," said Drakey Lakey.

Soon they met Goosey Loosey, who was standing by a stream.

"Honk! Honk!" she said in surprise. "Are you off to a party? Can I come too?"

"No, you silly goose, the sky is falling down," said Drakey Lakey.

"Goodness gracious! How did you know?" asked Goosey Loosey.

"Chicken Licken saw it," said Ducky Lucky.

"We're rushing off to tell the king," said Henny Penny.

"I'll go along too! Dear, dear me!" honked Goosey Loosey, as she ran behind them.

They passed Gander Lander. He was scratching about in the grass, looking for food.

"Come along now," said Goosey Loosey. "There's no time to waste."

"Why? What's happened? What's the matter?" asked Gander Lander.

"Don't you know that the sky is falling on our heads?" said Goosey Loosey. "Look, all of them are rushing off to tell the king."

"Wait for me. I want to come along," said Gander Lander.

So Goosey Loosey and Gander Lander quickly waddled along behind the others.

They went down a hill and were hurrying along when they met Turkey Lurkey.

"Well, well, so you're having a race, are you?" he said. "Who's winning?"

"Don't be silly," quacked Ducky Lucky. "We're not running a race!"

"The sky is falling down," Henny Penny told Turkey Lurkey.

"I don't believe it," said Turkey Lurkey.

"It's true, I saw it," said Chicken Licken. "A piece of it fell on my head."

"We're off to tell the king. He will know what to do," said Cocky Locky.

"Do you know where the king lives?" asked Turkey Lurkey.

"No, I don't, but Henny Penny does," said Cocky Locky.

"I don't know where the king lives," said Henny Penny. "Drakey Lakey does."

"No, no, I don't know where he lives. But I asked Chicken Licken. He said the king lives in the middle of the forest," said Drakey Lakey.

"Well, I think I'll come along, too," said Turkey Lurkey.

So he ran along behind Goosey Loosey and Gander Lander.

All the birds ran through the forest, looking for the king. By now they were tired and thirsty.

"Are you sure this is the way?" asked Goosey Loosey.

"No, I'm not," replied Gander Lander. "I do hope we are not lost."

"I have never come so deep into the forest before," said Drakey Lakey.

"Have you ever met the king?" asked Turkey Lurkey, as he ran along behind them.

"No, I haven't," said Drakey Lakey. "But I'm sure Chicken Licken has met the king. That's why he's rushing off to tell him."

Cocky Locky and Henny Penny were feeling very tired.

"Can't we stop and rest for a while?" asked Henny Penny.

"Yes, we have been running for a long time," said Cocky Locky.

"How can you think of resting?" said Chicken Licken. "What if the sky falls on our heads when we are resting?"

"What do you think the king will do?" asked Cocky Locky.

"I don't know. He's the king, so I'm sure he'll think of something," said Chicken Licken.

As they hurried along, gasping and panting, they met Foxy Loxy. He was a cunning fox, and he always got a good meal for himself with his clever tricks.

As soon as Foxy Loxy saw all the birds rushing along, he said to himself, 'Here comes a hearty meal for me!'

When the birds came up to him, he asked, "Where are all of you going?"

"We are off to find the king," said Ducky Lucky. "The sky is falling down."

"Is that so? How do you know?" asked Foxy Loxy.

"Chicken Licken told us. He saw it with his own eyes," said Turkey Lurkey.

"Yes, a piece of it fell on my head," said Chicken Licken.

"Dear me!" said Foxy Loxy. "Then we must tell the king. Do you know where he lives?"

"No," said Chicken Licken. "But I think he lives in the middle of the forest."

"No, no, he lives in a cave. I'll show you the place," said cunning Foxy Loxy.

He led the way to his cave. As soon as all the birds went into the cave, he followed them and gobbled up all of them.

LEARN TO SAY THESE WORDS

forest	hurried
foolish	waddled
afraid	rushed
trembled	worse
thunder	swimming
wandered	surprise
juicy	honked
gobbled	believe
gasped	thirsty
scratching	hearty

CAN YOU NAME THESE PICTURES?

NEW DAWN PRESS, INC.
USA• UK• INDIA

NEW DAWN PRESS GROUP

Published by New Dawn Press Group
New Dawn Press, Inc., 244 South Randall Rd # 90, Elgin, IL 60123
e-mail: sales@newdawnpress.com

New Dawn Press, 2 Tintern Close, Slough, Berkshire, SL1-2TB, UK
e-mail: ndpuk@newdawnpress.com

New Dawn Press (An Imprint of Sterling Publishers (P) Ltd.)
A-59, Okhla Industrial Area, Phase-II, New Delhi-110020
e-mail: info@sterlingpublishers.com; www.sterlingpublishers.com

So much to Read
Delightful Stories

All rights are reserved. No part of this publication may be reproduced, stored in a retrieval system or transmitted, in any form or by any means, mechanical, photocopying, recording or otherwise, without prior written permission of the publisher.

Published by Sterling Publishers Pvt. Ltd., New Delhi-110020.
Lasertypeset by Vikas Compographics, New Delhi-110020.
Printed at Sai Early Learners (P) Ltd., New Delhi-110020.